A FRIEND WORTH HAVING
AND OTHER STORIES

BY
CHINONYE ROSEMARY ENWEMADU

Copyright © 2024 by Chinonye R Enwemadu

A FRIEND WORTH HAVING AND OTHER STORIES

All rights reserved. No part of this publication may be reproduced, distributed, or transmitted in any form or by any means, including photocopying, recording, or other electronic or mechanical methods, without the prior written permission of the publisher, except in the case of brief quotations embodied in critical reviews and certain other noncommercial uses permitted by copyright law. For permission requests, write to the publisher, addressed "Attention: Permissions Coordinator," at info@beyondpublishing.net

Quantity sales and special discounts are available on quantity purchases by corporations, associations, and others. For details, contact the publisher at the address above.

Orders by U.S. trade bookstores and wholesalers.
Email info@BeyondPublishing.net

The Author can be reached directly at BeyondPublishing.net

Manufactured and printed in the United States of America distributed globally by BeyondPublishing.net

New York | Los Angeles | London | Sydney
ISBN Soft cover: 978-1-63792-780-9
ISBN Hardcover: 978-1-63792-779-3

Dedication

This book is dedicated to my dad, Engr. T.I.C Ukejianya (July 28, 1934 - August 22, 2024), who was an avid reader and whose love for knowledge and wisdom inspired me every day. He left behind an inspiring legacy and his memory will forever be cherished.

CONTENTS

A Friend Worth Having	5-16
A Pride That Destroys	17-24
A Wrong Choice	25-36
The Honest Beggar	37-49
Put Your Best Foot Forward	50-58

A FRIEND WORTH HAVING

Chioma lived with her parents in Onitsha. She was 14 years old and was an only child. Chioma's parents trained her to have good morals and to be respectful. She was used to the chaotic city, known for trade and commerce. The Onitsha market was the biggest market in Africa. There was rarely anything a person would want that could not be found there. She was quite happy living in Onitsha because it was the place of her birth, and her friends all lived there.

One day, her father came home and announced to his family that, they would be relocating to Lagos. His office had promoted him and given him a new position in their Lagos branch. Chioma received the news with mixed feelings. She was glad that her father had been promoted but she was unhappy because she would have to leave her friends in Onitsha behind. She wondered about Lagos. She was not sure about how she would settle into a new life in Lagos. Ijeoma and Fatima, her friends had hugged her profusely promising her that they would stay in touch. Her parents assured her that she would make new friends in Lagos. So, Choma felt better and looked forward to moving to Lagos with her parents.

The trip to Lagos was quite tiring, but she was thrilled about the upbeat city. On arriving in Lagos, her parents enrolled her in a new school. It was a private secondary school, Edison Secondary School. It was much bigger and more beautiful than her former school in Onitsha. Most of the students were children from rich homes and carried fancy bags – obviously bought on foreign trips on holidays.

Chioma's class was SS 1A. She settled into her new class but soon found that her new school was more academically advanced than her former school in Onitsha. She was a brilliant girl and knew that she would have to work extra hard to succeed.

While she set to work studying her books, she was yet to make friends with anyone. A sense of inferiority gripped her when she attempted to say 'hello' to the students. Some of them spoke with foreign accents and they all seemed to have their comfortable cliques and groups. One day, while sitting in her class and feeling lonely, a girl walked up to her. "Hi. My name is Ronke," she said. "I can show you around the school if you want and share some of my lesson notes with you. You can go through them at home. This will give you an idea of the topics we had covered before you joined the school."

Chioma's eyes lit up with delight. She was so happy. Now she had a friend she could be with. They soon struck up a conversation and before long, it seemed that they had known each other forever. Chioma and Ronke went everywhere together. They studied together and ate at the same table in the cafeteria. Chioma was able to catch up with lessons she had lost and became one of the top three in her class.

One day, while Chioma was in the cafeteria waiting for Ronke she heard a group of girls discussing at the next table. They had brought their phones to school and were engrossed with some app on their phone-screens. They were beautiful. They seemed to be from well to do homes with their well braided hair, expensive looking school bags and wrist watches. They wore amazingly short skirts. Most importantly, they were the happening girls in her form. She longed to be in their midst. One of them gesticulated animatedly and Chioma listened as the girl loudly informed her friends about a party she was planning in her house at the end of the month. Chioma knew the name of the girl talking. She was Moji, her classmate.

She secretly desired to be friends with these girls. Just then, Ronke arrived at the cafeteria. Chioma asked her about the girls sitting at the next table." Hmmm!" Ronke sighed. "Those girls act like they are untouchables. They are snobs and are rude even to teachers because they believe they can get away with anything, just because their parents are quite influential in society."

When Chioma got home, she kept thinking about those girls and longed to be in their clique. She liked Ronke, but Ronke was just nice and ordinary. She was not from a rich home and her parents didn't even have a car.

In her former school in Onitsha, Chioma had been one of the students everyone looked up to both for her brilliance and trendiness. Her parents were comfortable middle-class earners but gave her everything she wanted because she was an only child. This made other students think she was from a wealthy home. In her new school in Lagos, no one regarded her, except Ronke. She wanted to stand out like the girls in Moji's clique.

The next day, when she got to school, she walked up to Moji and introduced herself, "Hi. My name is Chioma. I love your hair band. I have one just like that at home." Moji looked at her snobbishly, without saying a word. Chioma felt quite humiliated and quietly went to her seat. Maybe if she showed these girls that she was cool, they would want to be her friends. She thought about Ronke. She was a nice girl but didn't have the looks and coolness that these other girls displayed with ease. So, she avoided Ronke for that day and wouldn't even walk with her to the cafeteria. She felt, if she was always seen with Ronke, the other girls would not want to be her friend, because Ronke was not cool. Ronke noticed her friend's strange behaviour and asked, "Are you okay Chioma? Is there something wrong?"

"I am fine," Chioma replied. "I just have a lot on my mind. I will see you later." When Chioma's mum came to pick her up from school, she begged her to get her a new beautiful school bag and a wristwatch. "What do you need a new bag for?" "Oh Mom, my bag's zips are all faulty and my books stick out," Chioma lied to her mother. So, her mother took her to a shop immediately and got her a new school bag and a wristwatch. She also begged her mother to buy her a deodorant. Her mother consented just to indulge her daughter and make her happy. When they got home, her mother advised, "Chioma, remember who you are and how your parents raised you. Please always be of good behaviour and make friends with people who give you good advice and help you to be a better person. Avoid people with bad character."

"Yes mum," Chioma replied.

On getting to school the next day, Chioma took the deodorant her mum bought for her and walked up to Moji. "Hello," she said. "I got this for you." Moji stared at Chioma in surprise and a smile lit her face, "Oh thank you. Would you like to join my friends and I for lunch at the cafeteria? "she offered.

Chioma had to keep herself from showing her excitement. She almost jumped. "Yes please, "she replied.

At break time, Ronke walked up to Chioma and asked if they could study together at the library after lunch.

"Sorry Ronke. I will be busy. Maybe another day," Chioma quipped feeling a twinge of guilt. "Couldn't Ronke see that she didn't fit her status?" she reasoned within herself.

Ronke looked at her oddly for a moment, turned on her heels and walked away.

At lunch time, Ronke walked into the cafeteria to see Chioma huddled around a table with Moji's clique of girls eating together. They were laughing at something in a glossy mag, and she walked past them to the counter to order her lunch. Chioma pretended not to see her, but Ronke deliberately walked past the table to the one she had shared with Chioma. She felt so bad. She ate her lunch quietly, then headed for the library.

Chioma watched her leave and felt like scum for a moment, but her attention was soon diverted by Moji. Moji had introduced Chioma to the other girls and told them that Chioma would be part of their clique.

Rita, one of the girls had openly joked about her shoes, "If you are going to be part of us, you must change those shoes. Wow! Are they hand-me-downs or something? They look ugly and please do something better with your hair." The other girls had laughed but Moji quickly reminded them about Chioma's intelligence. They all knew that she would be helpful when it came to cheating on their tests and exams. So, they dropped the demeaning jokes.

Turning her pretty head towards Chioma, Moji asked, "Do you have a phone?" Chioma shook her head in shame. "Well," continued Moji in a matter-of-fact tone, "...tell your parents to get you a phone."

Sitting on the bench by the driveway after school, Chioma was deep in thought, when her mother came to pick her up. "What is wrong?" her mother asked.

"Mummy, can I please have new school shoes, beautiful ones. Also, I need a phone. Chioma's mother looked at her in disbelief.

"What has gotten into you? What do you need a phone for? And there is nothing wrong with your shoes." Chioma burst out crying. Her mother hugged her, "Why are you crying?"

"Some girls made fun of me, because I don't have a phone. They made fun of my hair and shoes."

"Chioma," her mother responded, "...never allow people to put you down. Don't let what people say get to you. Always remember who you are."
"But mummy," Chioma said in between sobs, "...everyone has a phone in my class except for me. I really would love a new pair of beautiful school shoes. Please mum!"

Her mother paused for a while. What was wrong with her child? And why was she suddenly so full of demands? "I will think about it," she said to her child.

That evening, she discussed it with her husband, "I hope Chioma is not being influenced negatively in this school. All a sudden, she makes demands and cares a lot about what people think. I hope she is mixing with the right people in her school."

Chioma's father decided to have a word with her. That weekend, he called her by her pet name, "My Chi," he said, "always remember these words, 'You don't do things because others expect you to do them, but you do things for the right reasons'. So, tell me, why are you suddenly interested in having a phone and new shoes?"

"My daddy," Chioma replied, "some of my classmates use their phones to communicate with others after school. They discuss class lessons, and I always miss out on this because I don't have a phone. And really Daddy, there are these beautiful shoes most girls in my school have. I want them not because others have them, but because they are beautiful, my daddy pleaseeee."

Her father smiled. Chioma had a special place in his heart. He dotted on his daughter and loved her very much. He would do anything to make her happy. Moreover, she had always been a child who made them proud. It wasn't so bad if she wanted some things which her peers had, he reasoned.

"Alright. What My Chi wants, she gets," he replied.

Later that day, Chioma went shopping with her mother. She got the shoes and smart phone she wanted. Chioma was beside herself with joy.

"Now those girls will know, I am cool," she thought to herself. On Monday, when it was time for school, Chioma put her phone in her bag without her parents' knowledge and her mother dropped her off at the drive in. Chioma walked briskly through the crowd of students milling around the school grounds and ran up the stairs to show Moji her new phone.

"Wow!" exclaimed Moji genuinely admiring Chioma's smartphone. It was set in a pink glass case, "What a beaut! We will exchange numbers. There is a math test today. Since we don't sit together, always check your phone. I will be sending you messages so that you can send the answers to me. You must be skillful about this, so you don't get caught," she finished.

Chioma was shocked at her words. When did the conversation go from being cool and pretty to cheating on a test? She knew that she should speak up and object to Moji's terrible suggestion, but she so, so wanted to be in Moji's good books and so she obliged.

The test was uneventful, but Chioms's heart pounded all the while she craftily texted the answers to Moji. She felt lucky that they were not caught because the teacher was not paying attention. Moji and Rita ran up to Chioma at lunch time, smiling and grateful. They intertwined their elbows and walked off to buy her some snacks. "What a brain Chioma was? A worthy investment," Moji thought. Chioma immediately forgot her doubts and fears and sucked in the attention and respect of Moji's clique. She really wanted their approval.

Ronke sat in class very sad. What had she done to Chioma to deserve this awful treatment? Chioma had stopped talking to her and didn't even want to be seen with her. She felt bad about it but decided to keep her distance.

When Chioma got home that day, she thought about how she cheated on the test and all the lies she had told her parents to get what she wanted. The girls in her group were all vain, only interested in material things. She thought about her kind friend Ronke. Moji had even banned her from speaking to Ronke. "How can you mix up with someone like Ronke? Can't you see how she looks and dresses?" Moji had scoffed.

"But Ronke had accepted me for who I am. I didn't have to lie to my parents or have certain things or look in a certain way to please her. She helped me with my studies," she thought to herself.

These other girls were always up to one mischief or the other, lying to their parents to get what they wanted, having boyfriends and cheating to pass their tests and exams. They were making her become everything she stood against. How would her parents feel when they found out the truth about the life she was now living? Chioma regretted getting close to these girls, but she was already part of them and feared what they would do to her, if she decided to leave them.

Two terms had passed, and it was now time for the third term exams. As usual, Moji had told Chioma to supply the answers to her through her phone.

The students sat in the class properly spaced out and mostly pensive. The teacher who was invigilating the exam shared the scripts to the students, started them on the paper and left the class to get something. Unknown to them, the teacher was standing by the window gazing at every student. Chioma looked around to ensure the coast was clear and as had become her usual practice, brought out her phone and started chatting with Moji, sending the exam answers to her.

The teacher saw her, slunk in from the back door and caught her unawares. Chioma's heart sank, and blood drained from her face.

"What are you doing? "the teacher asked. "N-nothing," her voice quivered.

"Why is your hand in your bag?" the teacher asked sternly and placed her hand in the bag. She whipped out Chioma's phone. She read through the chat between Chioma and Moji. Immediately, she rounded up both and bundled them to the Principal's office. At this point, Chioma knew she was in trouble. Humbled and ashamed, Chioma wept before the Principal and confessed all her misdeeds. " Punish me sir, "she pleaded tearfully, "but please don't tell my parents. I cannot bear the look on their faces when they find out."

The Principal nodded gravely. He had seen this play out one too many times - the victims of negative peer pressure. "Unfortunately, I must tell them Chioma, You should have thought about this before doing what you did. I hope you learn your lesson."

Moji stood unrepentant before the Principal. Immediately, she denied Chioma.

"I don't know what she is talking about. I never asked her for answers, if she decided to send answers to me, I never asked her. I did not even check my phone to see what she sent."

Chioma looked at Moji in disbelief, "I thought we were friends." Moji stared sat her coldly and replied, "You are not and can never be my friend. What would I want with a girl like you? Chioma wept. "What had she gotten herself into?"

Fortunately, Moji was not that smart. Investigations from the smartphone revealed that she had indeed read the chat during the exams and had not objected to receiving the texts from Chioma. Other classmates also bore witness to their awkward activities during tests and exams.

Chioma's parents were called in and informed about what their daughter had done. Her parents were ashamed and heartbroken. On the way home, neither said a word to each other. When they got home, Chioma quickly went on her knees, crying and pleading with her parents for forgiveness.

"I don't know what got into me," she said, "Please forgive me. I will never do it again."

Her parents seized her phone and all the new things they had bought for her. At first, the school had said, she and Moji would be expelled, but later, they gave them the condition that to continue in the school, they had to repeat SS1 when the new term starts. Her parents accepted the conditions. Chioma begged her parents not to let her go back to that school, she couldn't bear the shame. Her parents insisted that she must go back and face the consequences of her actions. Moji's parents withdrew her from the school, standing by their daughter's claim that she hadn't cheated.

When the new term started, Chioma watched her classmates move on to

SS 2 while she had to repeat SS1. The first person to come to see her was her friend, Ronke. She felt too ashamed to face her.

Ronke hugged her. "I am sorry you must repeat the class, but don't worry, you are a smart girl, you will get over this. It is just a temporary setback."

Chioma could not believe her ears. "Ronke," she said with tears in her eyes, "...you are here, not regarding how I treated you. Can you ever forgive me? Ronke hugged her again.

"We may be in different classes, but I will always be your friend. We can go to the cafeteria together during break and study in the library together during our free time. I just want you to know that you can always count on me."

Chioma was happy and grateful to God. She may have lost her dignity and had to repeat a class, but she did not lose her friend. Most importantly, she had learned her lesson the hard way. And so, she and Ronke continued as friends until Ronke graduated from the school.

Moral of the story: Always listen to good advice and keep away from bad company.

A PRIDE THAT DESTROYS

Chidi was a strong boy who lived in Umuahia, in the eastern part of Nigeria. His father was a hard-working farmer and his mother, a trader. He had an older brother, Chijioke, who was meek, quiet and studious. Chidi was a 16-year-old who had unusual strength. He was unafraid of anyone or anything. His mother would often boast that her son is a reincarnation of her late father, who was a famous hunter and a very strong man in his time.

Chidi became so popular for his strength, that the villagers nick named him 'Agu' meaning lion. Boys – young and old, avoided him because he would easily challenge them to a fight and win.. While Chidi was strong and loud, Chijioke was meek and quiet. He was soft spoken and hated fighting or arguing with anyone. He would rather give in just to avoid trouble. Boisterous Chidi was constantly furious with his elder brother. "Why do you act so spineless?" he would ask Chijioke. " Can't you be bold for once in your life?"

Chijioke would rather walk out of the room when Chidi started with his taunts. He knew he was no match for his younger brother. Chidi had beaten him so many times and he did not want any more embarrassment.

This worried his father. "Show some respect to your elder brother," he would scold. "You should not be so reckless and disrespectful of others because of your strength." Chidi's father was proud of his son's strength, but he was not happy about his boastful and rude nature. He would often complain to his wife.

"You should not encourage Chidi's rudeness. His strength has gotten to his head. I fear that it will be his downfall one day."

Chidi's mother was happy about her son's strength and boasted about it to her friends in the market. "My boy must be the strongest boy in the village."

One day, Chidi and his brother Chijioke had an argument. As usual, temperamental Chidi rushed at his brother to beat him up. At that point, their mother walked in. "What is going on here?" she shouted. She looked at her younger son's arms akimbo and his muscled chest heaving beneath his light singlet. He looked like a wrestler. She began to worry about this unbridled strength. She looked at her first son and he lowered his eyes in humiliation.

"Chidi, you should respect your elder brother. Why should you humiliate him this way, because you are stronger?" Chidi apologized to his mother and brother. Chidi was fond of his mother. She was always kind to him and most times let him get his way. He did not want her to be angry with him.

When Chidi's father got back home in the evening, his wife greeted him and drew him away to their bedroom. "I now understand all that you have been saying about Chidi. I am afraid his hot headedness will ruin him one day and I don't know how to help him."

Later that evening, Chidi's father sent for his two sons and sat them down. He had told them the story of the book, "Things fall apart" by Chinua Achebe, and the heroic things, Okonkwo, one of the characters in the book had done. He cleared his throat and looked at Chidi, "It is a great thing to display strength my son and take pride in your God given gift. However, strength without control can ruin a person. You were not given strength to go about daring people and humiliating them. You should use your strength for more positive things."

Chidi went from his father's presence unperturbed. "Of what use is my strength, if I cannot show it off?" he thought to himself. "I want to be feared and known as a great person everywhere I go," he said under his breath as he walked off.

Even though Chidi's peers feared him, he did not have friends. Parents in the village asked their children to avoid Chidi because of his character and temperament. He was rude and aggressive even to his elders. People would complain to his parents who would apologize on Chidi's behalf.

One day at the village square, where boys played football, Chidi's team lost to Ude's team. Ude was happy and went round congratulating his teammates. This infuriated Chidi. Without warning, Chidi rushed at Ude and hit him hard such that he fell to the ground groaning. Every boy on the football field was appalled, but none could dare Chidi because they did not want to be in Ude's shoes. Ude's teammates, picked him up and helped him home. Some men who were passing by, confronted Chidi. Chidi refused their correction. "Eh hen? Even if they won, why should Ude rub it in?" he said trying to justify his actions. "If he tries it next time, I will beat him again."

The older men shook their heads in disappointment and went away.

Chidi's father was distraught when he heard the news of another injured victim of his son's bullying. "If you don't have a spirit of sportsmanship, then please don't play with others," Chidi's father scolded him tiredly. Chijioke had reported to his parents what Chidi did to Ude.

His father insisted, "We are going to Ude's house, and you must apologize to him and his parents."

Chidi reluctantly went with his father to Ude's house. He could not dare stand up to his father. At Ude's house, after Chidi apologized, Ude's mother begged Chidi's father, "Please ask your son to stay away from my son. I know he is strong and can defeat a whole village, but he should be careful. I will let this pass now, the next time, I will not take such behaviour lightly."

As Chidi and his father walked the bushy path home from Ude's house, his father kept thinking about how he could tame his son. "How else can I help this boy?" he thought sadly to himself.

Soon the festive period drew near, schools vacated for the term. During the Christmas season, boys and girls, young men and women would go to the village square. There were so many interesting things to see then. People who were based in the big cities like Lagos: and even those overseas, came home in December. This made the village an interesting place to be. Young men dressed in their best to woo the ladies; and the ladies took it a notch higher trying to outdo themselves in the latest fashion. On December 26th, universally known as Boxing Day, a day after Christmas, the village square was full. Music from the local disc jockeys livened the air. Traders offered tasty treats to the fun seeking crowd in the busy square. Boys and girls lazily milled around talking, laughing and generally enjoying one another's company.

Chidi had no close friends as no one wanted to associate with him, so he went out in the company of his older brother and his friends. While they were walking about, Chidi saw some of his mates with Ude. Ude was quite popular in school. Chijioke noticed that there was a stranger in their midst. Ude and his friends were talking to some girls, some of whom he recognized. They all seemed to be having fun. Chidi longed to be among them. However, he knew they would not want him there, so he decided to force himself in. "After all," he thought,"no one could confront him or dare tell him to leave."

So Chidi arrogantly walked into Ude's group and sat in their midst without greeting anyone. Silence fell on the group. Some of them became fearful of trouble breaking out because that almost always happened wherever Chidi went.

The new boy was having none of this rudeness. "Who invited you here?" he asked challenging Chidi.

Ude turned to him to calm frayed nerves, "Calm down Ibe. Please I don't want any trouble. Let's just leave."

Chidi was cross. "You obviously do not know who I am. How dare you open your dirty mouth to talk to me?" he asked the new boy now identified as Ibe.

Chijioke saw Chidi from a distance and quickly walked up to him, "Chidi!" he shouted, "Let's go home. Don't start any trouble now. This is not a place to fight."

Chidi refused to listen to his brother. He walked up to Ibe and standing head-to-head, and shoulder to shoulder with him, shoved him with his chest, daring him. "I am talking to you."

The girls sensing trouble moved a safe distance away from the scene appealing to Chidi to leave Ibe alone.. People gathered to the scene. Chidi saw this and desired to disgrace Ibe in the presence of everyone, for daring to confront him.

Ibe was Ude's maternal cousin. Ibe and his family were based in Lagos and had just come home for the Christmas celebration. Ibe was also a very strong boy. He was 14 years old, two years younger than Ude and Chidi, but he was tall. Ibe tried to listen to Ude and started walking away when Chidi pushed him.

Ibe moved so fast that Chidi did not see him coming. He lifted Chidi off the ground and threw him to the floor. Everyone in the village square stood stunned. No one had ever been able to stand up to Chidi, let alone overpower him. Chidi, obviously shocked, quickly stood up and rushed headlong at Ibe. Ibe tripped him with his foot, picked him up again and threw him to the ground.

Chidi was breathless. Trying to catch his breath he felt Ibe's weight on him and felt hammer-like punches on his face and body. Ibe forced Chidi's mouth open and filled it with lumps of sand from the ground. Chidi had been shamed at the village square. He cried and squealed for mercy. Ude and his friends quickly pulled Ibe off Chidi and begged him to spare him.

Ibe got up and walked out with Ude and his companions, the crowd cheering on and booing Chidi. Chidi was too ashamed to get up. He lay on the floor trying to get the gritty sand out of his bleeding mouth. He felt pains all over his body. His brother Chijioke, walked up to him and helped him home. He silently hoped that his brother had learned his lesson.

News had already reached Chidi's mother at the market, as women could not wait to tell her how her son was defeated by a Lagos boy. She quickly closed her shop and rushed home. Seeing Chidi's condition, she took him to the hospital where the doctor cleaned his wounds and put a big plaster on his head. On hearing the news, Chidi's father rushed to the hospital to see his son. Chidi felt humiliated. Chidi's father sensed that the boy had already been disgraced enough and did not want to rub it in but asked gently about how he was feeling. Chidi could not respond. Instead, hot tears streamed down his cheeks. His father gently touched him and said, "Don't worry, son. You will get over this. I hope you have learnt your lesson my boy. Strength is not necessarily the absence of weakness, but the ability to walk away even when confronted."

Chidi's parents had warned him several times and he had not listened. Elders in the village had chastised him over and over, but he had ignored their warning. Now he would have to live with this shame for a long time. Everyone in the village would taunt him. His ego had been dented by a boy younger than himself. He should have walked away when he had the chance, but his pride got the better of him and now that pride had brought him shame.

Moral of the story

Pride goes before a fall. Natural abilities given to us are not to be used to oppress people but help them.

A WRONG CHOICE

David watched the fly on the wall through a blur of tears. The stench of urine assaulted his nose, and the occasional mosquito whizzed past his ear to remind him that he was far from the comfort of home. " Oh my God!" he pleaded, "Please get me out of here." How did he get here? How did he get it so wrong? At what point did he derail so badly to get to this point of no return. With tears streaming down his face, he remembered how it all started. "My name is Rosemary, but you can call me Rosie".

David was born into a wealthy family. At the age of 5, David and his family relocated to the United States of America. David's parents decided that when he turned 14, he would return to Nigeria to complete his secondary education before returning to the US for his university education. This, they hoped, would help David imbibe more of the Nigerian culture and mature into a responsible young adult. David was to live with his grandmother, who resided in Port Harcourt.

When David clocked 14, he and his parents came to Nigeria, and after spending the holiday, his parents left for the US leaving him with his grandmother. David was enrolled into an expensive private school. He loved his school; the structures were like those in his Junior high school in the US and one could tell that only children from privileged homes attended the school. David's parents wanted him in the boarding house, but his grandmother decided against it saying she wanted to monitor him better. His grandmother had a driver and stewards.

Every morning, David prayed with his grandmother, and some evenings after school, he joined his grandmother to attend Christian fellowships. David's grandmother was a devout Christian and had raised her children this way. She wanted David to be firmly rooted in the Christian doctrine.

David started school and was placed in SS1A. He made friends easily because he was a well-mannered boy and people were attracted to his American accent. David was also intelligent and did well in his studies. One day, he went to the school cafeteria for lunch. While eating, he noticed a beautiful girl seated at the next table chatting with her friends. He stared at her with admiration.. Almost as if she was alerted by his gaze, she turned towards him and her eyes met his. She smiled at him and returned to her conversation with her friends. He soon found out that she was in SS1C.

David had a neighbor, Ada. Ada lived with her parents and attended the same school as David. Ada and her parents also worshipped in the same church as David's grandmother, so in no time, David and Ada had become good friends. Ada was in SS2 and was a year older than David and would refer to him as her younger brother.

One day, as David sat in the library revising for his Physics test, the girl he had seen in the cafeteria, walked up to him. "Hi," she said, "my name is Rosemary, but you can call me Rosie. What is your name?" David was a bit embarrassed by her boldness. "My name is David," he responded. She smiled and pulled a chair to sit by him. "I love the way you talk," she said.

He was taken aback. "Was she flirting with him?" He took a fresh look at her. Her hair was long and silky, her face was pretty and her skin glowed. She had a brazen confidence about her.,

The bell for the next period rang and she stood up to go. "Can we talk after school?" she asked. School closed at 3.30pm, and David always left early in order not to keep his grandmother's driver waiting, but here was this beautiful girl, he would definitely love to stay back for a few minutes to chat with her. He knew his grandmother would be upset if he came home late, so he replied, "Maybe another day. I must go home early. I have fellowship after school."

"Oh really?" she responded. "Alright. Some other time. She turned and walked away.

After fellowship, David strolled to Ada's house and asked if she knew Rosemary. "Rosemary?" Ada gawked, "the girl is bad news. She keeps company with the worst of the worst. Please stay away from her." David was shocked. How could such a beautiful and friendly girl be bad news? All night, he thought of an excuse to tell his grandmother to justify coming home late the next day - after all, there was no fellowship.

Irrespective of Ada's warning, he was more intrigued with Rosemary than ever.

The next day, before leaving for school, David told his grandmother, that he had extra lessons with his Physics teacher after school. This wasn't true but his unsuspecting grandmother believed him.

After school that day, he sought out Rosemary and found her in the midst of her friends. There was something odd about this company of boys and girls. She beckoned on him to join them. He sat in their midst for a few minutes but felt uncomfortable with their discussion. He told her that he had to go home and left.

When he got home, he thought about what Ada had said about Rosemary, "She is bad news." Rosie's friends had talked about films, which were inappropriate for their age and their obscene jokes seemed a norm among them. David decided to get Rosie off his mind. "I can't be friends with such a person," He thought to himself. He even had to tell a lie to his grandmother just to see her after school. He was not comfortable with this.

The next day, Rosie came to David's class to see him.

"Why did you leave like that?" she asked with a pout. He tried to find an excuse and before he could come up with something, she said, "I understand - My friends and I are too unchristian for you. We can hang out after school today and you can tell me about some things you learn in fellowship. I can even visit you at home."

David looked at her and nodded, "Okay," he said. He just could not understand why he found it difficult to stay away from her. After school, he dropped his bag in the car and begged the driver to give him 10 minutes. He went to Rosie's class to look for her. He found her alone in class and he stayed awhile chatting with her. He told her about his childhood, and she did same. She was quite a funny person, and he found himself laughing at her expressions. He felt bad about his initial judgment of her person. Time flew by. He looked at his watch and was quite surprised at how quickly time had passed.

"Can I visit you at home?" she asked him.

"Yes," he said and gave her his address.

She kissed him gently on the lips and left. He stood there in shock wondering what just happened. He knew in his heart that he should run without looking back, but he just couldn't get her off his mind.

David always told his grandmother everything that happened in school. He told her about his new friend Rosie, but left out the detail of the kiss, or what Ada had said concerning her. That weekend, Rosie's driver dropped her off at David's house. She wore a skimpy skirt and a top that almost revealed her navel. David's grandmother was uncomfortable with her dressing.

"Where are your parents?" she asked.

"My parents had to go out," Rosie responded.

Rosie spent almost the whole day with David. They watched TV and talked about different things. David noticed Rosie kept flirting with him. After a while, he asked if she was a Christian and went to church.

"We don't go to church in my house," she replied. "Will you please teach me everything you know about the Christian religion? We can be very good friends," she continued.

When Rosie left, David's grandmother sat with him and said, "Listen to me my son. Evil company corrupts good character. Never make friends with people who exhibit questionable character. They will mar you. I am not comfortable with this friend of yours. Please stay away from her."

David knew his grandmother was right, just like Ada, his neighbor, but he liked Rosie. He liked her very much and the thought of not being her friend was just not acceptable to him. He tried to justify his reasons when he visited Ada in the evening.

"Rosie is not from a Christian home. We can't judge her dressing and the way she behaves when her parents did not teach her the right thing. David you can talk with her and help her as much as you can, but please know where to draw the line. Don't always be in a place with her alone."

David looked down, he remembered the kiss and understood what Ada was saying.

Weeks went by, and the term ended. Rosie had invited David to her house.

David knew there was no way his grandmother would permit him to visit Rosie, so he thought of a way of visiting her without his grandmother's knowledge. David had another friend in church Kamsy, who lived on his street. David begged Kamsy to cover for him, that he would tell his grandmother that he was visiting Kamsy. Kamsy was not thrilled with the idea but did not want to upset David, so he agreed. David knew that Ada would never cover for him, so he did not tell her about his plan.

"Grandma, I want to spend some time with Kamsy," he said.

"Alright. Don't stay out too long," she responded. David had some pocket money and boarded a taxi to Rosie's house. Rosie's parents were not home. A woman who was the nanny let him in, and he walked into the sitting room and found Rosie, with her same group of friends from school, smoking and dancing. Rosie was shocked to see David, as he did not inform her that he was coming. She walked out of the group and hugged and kissed his lips.

"Darling," she drawled, "you did not tell me you were coming." She smelled of alcohol. Her eyes looked quite glazed over and he was certain she was under the influence of alcohol or maybe some drug. "What are you doing?" he asked in disbelief. At this, her friends started laughing.

"We were just having a party," she replied.

"Where are your parents?" he asked.

"They are not around." She said.

Hard core rap music blared from the sound system in her living room and the entire scene looked like a club. He told her he had to leave, but she held on to him and begged him not to go. She took him to her room, and explained that, she and her friends were just playing around. They were not doing anything bad.

"Rosie," he replied, "this is not right - your dressing and the way you and your friends act. It is so inappropriate."

She went on her knees and begged him not to stop being her friend.

"You are one of the most important persons in my life. David felt bad for her. I must go now, since you are with your friends. I can come and visit you next week." She agreed and he left.

David got back home and thought of the scene at Rosie's house.

How could he stay away from her? He knew that he himself was compromising his faith by telling lies to be with her and allowing her to kiss him. He was yielding to sin but refused to face up to that. He lied to himself by pretending that he wanted to help her when he himself was falling.

" Everything about her was strange - her choice of friends, her dressing and where were her parents, by the way?" he wondered.

She had said that he was important to her. Maybe she simply needed the right company, and she would change and become better.

"But who is influencing who?" a still small voice spoke in his heart. David ignored the question.

So, every now and then, he would visit Rosie in her house, while his grandmother believed he was visiting Kamsy. He never met her parents on any of those visits.

School resumed and David, still found time to be with Rosie. He liked her a lot. The other boys in her group just felt he was just a naive boy who knew nothing. One day, Rosie and her female friends were invited to a party. The party was organized by some male university students. Rosie knew one of the organizers Kenny and was close to him. At the party, Kenny took Rosie and her friends to a room and offered them drinks. Unknown to Rosie and her friends, their drinks were drugged. The girls were raped and left in the room to sleep off. The girls woke up later when the party was over and realized what had happened to them. When they got to school on Monday, they reported the incident to their male friends. Together, they planned on their revenge. Rosie did not inform David.

By the weekend, Rosie invited Kenny to her house. David had also planned to visit Rosie, but forgot to let her know that he was coming and decided to surprise her. Kenny oblivious of what was planned went to Rosie's house only to meet some boys in her house. They quickly descended on Kenny and started hitting him with sticks. One of them brought out a knife and stabbed Kenny at his side. At this point, David walked in to see the horrid scene. Rosie was surprised to see David.

"What are you doing here?" she asked him pensively.

"I just wanted to visit," he stammered, "What is going on here?" David was scared. What had he walked in on? - A murder scene? Oh no!

Rosey pulled his arm, "Please be quiet. Just come to my room."

"No!" he shouted. "I need to leave now."

"You are not going anywhere," one of the boys responded. "Just sit quietly and keep your mouth shut."

David was trembling and wondering what he got himself into. His palms were sweaty and unsteady.

Suddenly, there was the noise of Police sirens. A black Police van with two other cars on its tail parked in front of Rosie's house. Rosie's neighbor had heard the commotion and saw the boys who went into the house and decided to call the Police. This was a GRA (Government Reserved Area), and they had a Police station nearby. The Police men forced their way into the house and saw Kenny bleeding on the floor. Two of them tried to stabilize Kenny and called for an ambulance, while the other policemen arrested everybody in the house. David shouted as he was shoved into the van, "I am innocent! I did not do anything! I am not part of them. Rosie, please tell them."

No one listened to him.

At the Police station, they all wrote their statements and were locked up in cells. Their parents and guardians were contacted. David sat in the cell amidst the smell of urine, mosquitoes and ruffians. He had been stripped to his singlet and boxers. Tears streamed down his eyes as he wondered about his fate. Would that poor boy they stabbed survive? Would he be imprisoned for a crime he did not commit?

Rosie's nanny came to the station to stand in for her parents as she explained that Rosie lived with her mother who was divorced, and her mother was out on a business trip. She did not have Rosie's father's contact. The other students' parents came, and David spotted his grandmother among them. He felt so ashamed and could not face her. Luckily for him, the neighbor who called the Police came to the station to give her statement and explained that the commotion in the house had started before David arrived in the house. It was at this point that David was let out on bail. News came from the hospital that Kenny was out of harm's way, but still needed treatment because the knife wound was deep. He had sustained serious injuries from the beatings he received.

All the way home in the car with his grandmother, David did not say a word. His grandmother cried.

"Where did I miss it, David?" she asked. "You lied to me. You said you were visiting Kamsy. I had warned you to stay away from that girl. You deceived me. How could you?"

David was so ashamed and kept sobbing all the way home. When they got home, he went on his knees and held his grandmother.

"Please forgive me grandma. I lied to you. I don't know what came over me. I liked Rosie and thought that I only wanted to help her. I deceived myself that with good company, she could become a better person, but I lied to myself. I was attracted to her. Grandma, please forgive me. I will never deceive you again."

When David got to his room, he sat on his bed and thought about all that had happened. What a fool he had been? Rosie deceived him all this time. She was not interested in being better. She enjoyed her lifestyle. How could she and her friends stab that young man? Were they planning to kill him or what? Could teenagers be that dangerous?

Now he understood, What Ada meant when she said Rosie was bad news. Rosie had not cared to defend him when he needed her. She had been willing to let him get punished for a crime he did not commit. But for Rosie's neighbor who spoke up for him, he would not have been granted bail. He was so afraid. He would have thrown away his life over a girl who was not genuine. David made a resolve never to fall into this temptation again. He will listen to sound advice and never tell lies anymore.

Moral of the story

The wrong choices we make, may come back to haunt us.

THE HONEST BEGGAR

In the city of Kano, there lived a poor man Musa. He had a wife and several children. Their youngest son Aminu was a bit crippled on one foot and could only walk with the support of a stick. This was so because when Aminu was an infant, his mother carried him on her back to fetch water from the village stream, and as she bent over the river, Aminu fell from her back. This affected his right foot.

His parents were too poor and so could not afford medical help. They relied on the village native doctor who massaged Aminu's foot every now and then, but that did not help. Aminu's parents could not afford to educate any of their children and so every day they wandered about each trying to fend for themselves.

Aminu had a good friend, Dambala. Dambala had a hunch back. Dambala suggested that they should start begging on the streets, and so every day, Aminu and Dambala would wander to a part of town and there beg for alms.

One day, Dambala visited Aminu in his house and suggested that they travel out of Kano to Lagos.

"My cousin who lives in Lagos just came home. He said there are lots of opportunities in Lagos. We can make more money begging on the streets and who knows, we may even get menial jobs," Dambala said.

Aminu was not thrilled with the idea of leaving home. "We don't know anyone outside Kano. How can we just travel to an unknown place?" Dambala replied, "We have been begging on the streets of Kano for years and yet have nothing. Why don't we take this chance? We have nothing to lose. If the place does not suit us, we can come back to Kano."

Aminu went home and thought about this all night. "Dambala is right. All I do here is beg. This is not the way I want to live my life. I am already 18 years old, and my parents have nothing to offer me."

By the next morning, when he met up with Dambala he had made up his mind. "I agree with you. I am ready to go, but where do we get the money to travel?"

"My uncle drives a trailer that carries goods to Lagos. With a small token, we can ride in the boot with the goods to Lagos," Dambala replied.

With their plan perfected, they set out for Lagos the following week. All through the ride, they marveled at what they saw on the road and were amazed that there was so much more going on outside their village in Kano. Each wondered in his heart what adventure awaited them in Lagos. The trailer they were travelling in broke down on the road and they had to pass the night in the city they were in. It had not been a comfortable journey so far. There were so many bumps on the road and squeezing in the open boot with the goods was not palatable, but they had no choice. They alighted from the trailer to stretch their legs and look for a spot on the road where they could pass the night. Aminu looked around in wonder. Things in this place seemed weird to him. Improperly dressed women threw themselves at men hoping to get some money off them. Some men sat in a corner smoking and drinking and laughing out loud. Aminu thought of his village in Kano. These things are forbidden. Those who engage in these acts hide themselves and do these things in secret. Aminu felt shocked and wondered if he could really fit into this new life he was envisaging in Lagos.

"Dambala!" he called out to his friend, "I hope Lagos will have good things in store for us and not end up being a bad decision on our part."

Dambala looked at his friend with a worried expression and responded, "I hope so too."

The next morning, with the trailer fixed, Aminu and Dambala continued their journey. They finally arrived in Lagos at midnight. Dambala's uncle took them to his friend Usman who sold tomatoes in one of the markets. "You can stay here for one week and then find your way. I hope your dreams are fulfilled in Lagos," he said to them and bade them farewell. The next day, Dambala's uncle set off for Kano.

They rested for two days in the house and on the third day, set out with Usman to his shop in the market. Usman introduced them to other young boys in the market. Most of them spoke the Hausa language like Aminu and Dambala. Some of them had one form of deformity or the other, while others were not physically challenged in any way, but still begged for alms from people who came to purchase things from the market. They would sometimes help people carry their goods to their cars for stipends. Aminu and Dambala were happy and started mixing with these young boys and quickly learned how to cope on the streets of Lagos. At night, they would sleep with these boys in some open shades in the market. They ate together and became part of a community that looked out for each other.

Weeks passed, and Aminu and Dambala had become accustomed to their daily routine. One of the big shops in the market was owned by Mr. Obi. Everyone in the market called him 'Ichie', a chieftaincy title he received from his village in Imo state. He was obviously a rich man. He had boys who served in his shop, and they all lived in the boy's quarters of his house. Some of the boys in Ichie's shop were friendly and chatted often with the Hausa boys when they were less busy. Sometimes, Ichie's son,

Eze, would visit his father's shop. Eze was nothing like his father who was humble and easy going. Eze was about Aminu's age, but he was pompous and overbearing. He looked down on the Hausa beggars like Aminu and Dambala and called them lazy.

"You came all the way from the north to beg for alms in Lagos, instead of working to earn a living. How can able bodied men like you beg for a living? Don't you have shame?

His words hurt Aminu and Dambala. Aminu had a close friend amongst Ichie's boys. His name was Igwe. He would complain to Igwe about Eze's insults.

"Don't mind him," Igwe replied. "He is privileged. His father has worked hard to provide for his family, so Eze and his siblings lack nothing. The boy thinks every other person who is not rich is just lazy. He also treats us who work for his father the same way, so don't worry. He is just ill mannered."

Eze had some friends with whom he would sometimes come with to his father's shop. They would sit around in a circle outside Eze's father's shop and drink and poke fun at some other traders in the market whose businesses were not doing so well. Aminu always avoided Eze especially when he was with his friends.

One day, a customer came to buy goods from Mallam Usman. The customer spent so much money that Aminu, Dambala and some other boys hovered around hoping to get alms from the customer, especially since she was Hausa like them. They offered to carry her goods to her car, and they scrambled to carry a piece of item hoping a tip would drop from the rich madam. Others, including Aminu, who were not fast enough to pick an item because of their disabilities, followed the woman to her car, praising her and begging for alms.

Eze and his friends were in his father's shop. They heard the commotion from the beggars and came out of the shop to see what the noise was all about. They watched the group of beggars returning with a hundred naira each, a gift from the generous woman. Eze shook his head in disgust and turned to his friends. "Look at this set of disgrace who call themselves men. All they do is beg and disturb people's peace. Can you go back to the holes you crawled out from?" Eze shouted at Aminu and his friends.

This upset the Hausa boys, and they charged towards Eze, who ran into his father's shop. There was so much noise in the market as the infuriated beggars threatened to deal with Eze and his friends. Ichie was not in the market that day, but his boys came out to confront the Hausa boys. Igwe, who was close to Aminu and Dambala, dragged them to the side and begged them to calm their friends down. Igwe apologized to the beggars and begged them to ignore Eze. Mallam Usman came to the scene and spoke to the boys in their language, asking them to go about their business and ignore Eze.

Mallam Usman and Ichie were good friends and always looked out for each other in the market. Ichie had complained about Eze's behaviour so many times to Mallam Usman. "He is my last son," he said, "but is nothing like his seniors. My other children are so responsible, have graduated from school and are already running their own businesses. Maybe, his mother and I spoilt him being the youngest and we did not realize when he degenerated this way."

Mallam Usman would console Ichie and remind him that all children are not the same. "Do your best," Mallam Usman told Ichie, "and let God take care of the rest. I am sure he will turn out right in the end."

Ichie told Mallam Usman that he had plans to send Eze to school abroad and was already processing his papers. Eze had gone to the UK embassy and had been granted his student visa.

His older brother, who was also a businessman, gave him a thousand pounds to congratulate him. Eze had also gone to some of his uncles and relatives and gotten cash gifts from them. Eze put the pounds, naira and his Nigerian passport containing his UK student visa in a brown envelope. In his usual manner, he gathered his friends for a feast just to brag. He told them about his forthcoming trip abroad and all the gifts he had received from relatives. Eze invited his friends to join him in his father's shop where he would order drinks and nkwobi for them. Eze could not contain himself as he bragged to his friends and the boys in his father's shop about how luck was on his side. "I was born into wealth, and I will die wealthy," he boasted. Aminu was in a corner observing the scenario. As Eze reached into his bag to pay for the Nkwobi dish, a brown envelope fell out of his bag. No one noticed except Aminu.

Aminu thought nothing of it and went about his business until it was time for the market to close. Eze and his friends entered his car and left. Ichie's boys also closed the shop and went home. As Aminu and Dambala were leaving, Aminu noticed the brown envelope was still on the floor. He went and quietly, picked up the envelope. It was bulky, but he chose not to open it. Aminu and Dambala in their usual style, went to Mallam Usman's shop to pass the night. Aminu waited for Damabala to sleep and quietly opened the envelope. He was shocked at what he saw. He saw a green booklet and some strange notes and naira notes. Aminu was afraid. He could hardly sleep that night. Early the next morning, he woke Dambala and showed him those things. They counted the naira notes, and it came to a hundred and twenty thousand naira. They looked at each other and laughed with joy.

Before Mallam Usman came to the shop, Aminu and Dambala left for another part of the market. There were some Hausa men who sold there too. Aminu went to one of them and showed him the foreign notes and green passport he had, asking if they were worth anything. The man told him, the foreign notes were pounds, British money and if he sold them, he could get a lot of money. The green booklet was a passport one uses to travel outside the country. Aminu thanked the man and lied that his uncle sent him on an errand and that he would return soon. Aminu and Dambala wandered on in the market now scared. They went to a corner to discuss.

"Do you know what this means?" Dambala asked. "Luck has shone on us. We came to Lagos to make money and did not know it would come to us so easy. Let us sell the pounds and the green booklet and with the naira we have, return to Kano to start a business."

This suggestion did not sit well with Aminu. He was poor, but his parents raised him well and taught him never to take things that did not belong to him. Aminu knew the envelope and the contents belonged to Eze. He struggled with his feelings. To buy time, he told Dambala that they would perfect their plans, and that they needed to plan better. Aminu and Dambala returned to Mallam Usman's shop and asked if they could pass the night in his house instead of sleeping in the shop. Mallam Usman was surprised but thought nothing of it and gave his permission.

Aminu and Dambala got to their room in Mallam Usman's house and hid the envelope in one of the cupboards. Dambala was happy and already planning what he would do with his own share of the money. Unknown to him, Aminu had his own internal battles. That night, Aminu could hardly sleep.

"I can't keep these items. That would be stealing," he thought to himself. "Eze is a mean boy who treats people badly. He does not deserve to be pitied, "he tried to justify not returning the money. What should he do? Would his conscience permit him to make use of resources he did not work for?

Eze went home and slept off after drinking with his friends. The next morning, he went to get the brown envelope from his bag only to discover it was no longer there. He was alarmed.

"Where is my passport? Where is my money?" he screamed as he searched the bag frantically for it. He searched everywhere in his room and by this time was terrified, angry and bewildered. He rushed to his car and searched every nook and cranny but found nothing.

How would he face his parents? What would he tell them? He drove to the market and ran into his father's shop shouting at the boys there. "Who stole my passport and my money? It was in my bag and one of you stole it. Give it back to me."

He was hysterical and was screaming.

"Calm down," Igwe said. "We can't even understand what you are saying. What passport? What money?" he asked.

"I had it in a brown envelope. It was in my bag, but it is no longer there." Igwe and the other boys started searching all over the shop for the items but found nothing. Aminu and Dambala had come to the market that day and heard the whole noise going on in Ichie's shop. Aminu knew what the matter was but said nothing. Eze threatened Igwe and the other boys. "I will report you to my father. You are all thieves. You will be sacked," he said as he stormed out of the shop to drive back home.

When Ichie learnt what happened, he felt very bad.

"What could I have done so wrong to be given a son like you?" he asked. "Can't you do anything right? Since you have misplaced your passport, then you will sit at home. No more travelling for you."

Eze felt his world crashing around him and cried all day.

"After boasting, what would his friends say?" he lamented. "Who could have done this to him?"

Ichie mandated Eze to apologize to the boys in the shop. "Since these boys started working for me, I have not lost anything. So, you cannot accuse them." Eze reluctantly apologized and his father told him, "No more lazying around. Every morning, you will join the boys to work in the shop and make yourself useful." This was a hard punishment for Eze. He avoided his friends. Now he resumed shop duties mopping the environment and taking stock of the inventory.

It was almost a week since Aminu found the envelope. Dambala was waiting for Aminu to make up his mind. "When are we going back home to Kano?" he asked.

Aminu looked at his friend and said, "It is true we came to Lagos to look for a livelihood, but this money and everything contained in the envelope does not belong to us. It belongs to Eze."

"And so, what?" Dambala retorted. "That ill-mannered boy should get what he deserves. He looks down on others. Let this be a lesson to him. If we go to Kano, nobody will ever trace us, and they will not know we took the money."

Aminu looked at his friend, "We may be poor beggars," he said, "but we are not thieves and will never steal anything from anyone."

That evening, Aminu went to Mallam Usman and told him how he found the brown envelope. After his narrative, he handed the envelope and its contents to Mallam Usman. Mallam Usman was surprised.

"You mean you choose to return this envelope to its owner? I know you have never liked that boy Eze, because of the way he treats you," he said.

Aminu smiled. "I will not steal to become rich. Instead, let me remain poor," Aminu concluded.

The next morning, Ichie was in his shop with his son Eze. the shop attendants were busy about their business when Mallam Usman walked in with Aminu.

"Ah Mallam my friend, how are you?" Ichie asked.

"I am fine," Mallam Usman responded taking a seat., "My boy here has something to tell you. Aminu handed over the brown envelope to Ichie and explained to him how the envelope had fallen from Eze's bag, and he had found it and chosen to return it, even though he struggled with this decision. Everyone present looked at Aminu in disbelief.

Ichie, cleared his throat and said, "You mean you found this envelope with all the money it contains and chose to return it?" He turned to Mallam Usman and said, "I would never have believed that we can still find young boys with integrity." Ichie turned to his son and asked, "Eze if the reverse was the case would you have returned this envelope to the owner?"

Eze shook his head indicating a 'no' with tears streaming down his face. He walked up to Aminu and knelt before him and said, "You are an honorable person. Please forgive everything I have said to you and your friends. Today I have learnt a hard lesson. Thank you for returning my envelope."

Mallam Usman turned to leave with Aminu. Suddenly, Ichie called them back and said, "Aminu, would you like to own a shop in the market? You can think of things you can sell in the shop."

Aminu looked at Mallam Usman in amazement and shouted for joy. He could not believe his ears. "Yes sir," he replied, a huge smile on his face. "If given the opportunity, I would love to own a shop and sell goods." Ichie nodded and said thank you again, and Mallam Usman, Aminu and Dambala left his shop.

One month later, Aminu and Dambala stood in their shop in the market. They were selling, onions, potatoes and yams. Dambala's uncle supplied them these food items from the north. Ichie had not only paid for the shop for Aminu and Dambala, he had also rented an apartment for them near the market.

One day, Aminu and Dambala closed their shop after the day's sales. Dambala was struck by their good fortune. It still felt like a dream to him. He turned to Aminu and said, "Thank you for choosing to do the right thing. We would never have been this peaceful and fortunate if we had kept back that money." Aminu replied," It pays to always do the right thing. We have come to Lagos, and we now have our own livelihood." The two friends finished locking up their shop and headed home.

Moral of the story

Being honest has its rewards and integrity always brings honor and goodwill.

PUT YOUR BEST FOOT FORWARD

Ade was born into a family of six. He was the first of four children. His parents were traders. Ade's siblings shone in their academics. They were consistently among the top three in their respective classes. Ade did not fare so well in his academics. He was always at the bottom of his class. He loved sports though and could be found playing a game of soccer with his friends as soon as he had the chance.

His father being a strict disciplinarian and lover of books found this disturbing. As a result of this, he often scolded and punished Ade because he thought he was quite unserious with his studies. He often compared him with his siblings.

"Your mother and I work hard to be able to train you and your siblings in school. Your siblings show appreciation by bringing good results home. You are good for nothing, always coming bottom three in your class. Why can't you be like your siblings and work harder at your studies? These were the words Ade had to put up with almost every day from his father. He always felt hurt when his father scolded him. He would have loved to make his parents proud, but he just didn't know how. Ade's mother was an understanding woman, but she was timid. She couldn't face her husband because of his strictness. She didn't like how her husband treated Ade, but she couldn't do anything about it, because she was afraid of what her husband might do if she talked to him about it. Usually, after one of his heated sessions of scolding or beating Ade, she would slip into his room to console him. "I know you are doing your best my son and I believe one day you will be great. You will see. Don't be discouraged."

Ade always felt better after listening to his mother, but in his heart, he knew she was just cheering him up. He never believed he could amount to anything in life.

His grandmother paid them frequent visits. Ade loved his grandmother. She was a patient and caring woman. She would quietly listen to all that her grandchildren had to say and give them good advice. She always had a blessing or prayer on her lips for all of them.

One day, after being scolded by his father, Ade went into his room to cry. Normally, he would go to the backyard to cry, because he shared a room with his siblings and would not want them to see him in that state. However, on this day, their father had decided to reward the other children's stellar performance in their exams, by taking them out to buy them clothes. The term had just ended, and Ade's siblings all scored above eighty percent in their results. Ade scored fifty percent. This was the least mark needed to be promoted to the next class.

"At least I was promoted to JSS 3. Why is father not satisfied with this?

Ade was so engrossed in his pain that he did not hear his grandmother come in. She walked into the room to see her grandson weeping. She felt so heartbroken.

"Ade, my son, what is the matter? Why are you crying?" she asked with great concern.

"Mami," he said in utter surprise. This was what she was fondly called by her children and grandchildren. "Sorry Mami, I didn't know the door was unlocked."

"Yes," she replied. "I was surprised to see the door open and no one in the sitting room. Where is everyone?

"My mum went to her shop, and daddy went out with my siblings," Ade replied. "Why didn't you go with them? Are you not feeling well? Why do you look so downcast my son?" Mami hobbled over to his bedside and sat beside him.

Ade could not control the tears anymore. He started crying again. "Mami, I do my best honestly, I do. I don't know why I can't get good grades like my siblings. At least I got a promotion. I scored fifty percent, and I am promoted to JSS 3, yet my father is never satisfied. He scolds and humiliates me in front of my siblings. He never acknowledges my efforts. Sometimes, Mami, I wonder if he is really my father." Mami nodded her head with understanding.

"Never say such words again Ade," his grandma said softly. She knew her son was a strict man, who drove his children hard, but she also knew he loved all his children and only wanted them to succeed and have a better life than he had. However, this time, he had gone too far. "Why exclude Ade from an outing with his siblings? This could lead to a rift in the family and Ade could feel unloved," she thought in her heart.

"Ade my son, don't cry," she said wiping his tears. "Remember that you are growing up to be a man. Men don't cry at little challenges. They face them squarely. You will prove to your father and everyone than you are not just good but the best."

"But how Mami?" he asked. "I struggle with my academics."

"You will need extra help," his grandmother counseled. "Moreover, apart from your academics, there are other things you are good at, like sports for instance. I have watched you play football. I see the skills you have there. You will work on every aspect of your abilities including your academics and you my son will stand out." Ade felt hope bubble within him. His eyes shone with excitement. He loved listening to her because she always had words of wisdom to share.

It was true he loved football, but his father had banned him from participating in any kind of sports until he improved on his grades. He wondered how would get back into playing the sport he loved. With Mami on his side though, his father may comply.

Mami rose from his bedside. "I will wait for your parents to come home, and I will speak to both of them today before I leave." Ade was hopeful. His father was a strict man, but if there was anyone who could stand up to him, it was Mami.

That evening when Ade's parents came home, Mami sent the children to their room. "I want to speak with your parents," she told Ade and his siblings.

"Mami, welcome." his father started, "I hope all is well. Why do you look so downcast?

"My son," Mami started, "I know you have good intentions towards your children, but I don't like the way, you treat your first son Ade." Ade's father responded, "But Mami, Ade is lazy. He is not making any efforts to improve."

"Then we will give him the extra help he needs," replied Mami. "Every child is not the same and children learn at different paces. We will hire a lesson teacher to help him with the subjects he struggles with."

Ade's parents agreed that this was a good idea and decided to get a lesson teacher for Ade. "One more thing," Mami added, "keeping him away from sports is not the solution. Let him do the sports he enjoys at school. Remember, there are different fields in which a person can excel." Ade's father was not happy with the suggestion of letting his son participate in sports, but he could not go against his mother's wish. "Alright Mami, I will do as you have said," he complied. "I only hope you are right in these suggestions you have proffered." Before Mami left the house, she prayed for her grandchildren and asked Ade to walk her to the bus stop.

On the way, she counselled Ade, "Listen my son, life brings many challenges, but we learn to face them bravely. Always learn to put your best foot forward." Ade was puzzled. He looked at his feet and wondered which was better. His grandmother smiled.

"Listen my son, there is a God given talent in everyone. When you find your talent, excel in it and showcase your talent. Do your best in your academics, always strive to be the best in all you do, and in the places where you can excel, don't just excel but shine." With these words, she kissed her grandson on the cheek and said goodnight.

Ade returned home pondering over his grandmother's words.

Ade's father went to the school to inquire about extra lessons for his son. The principal obliged and said that he could join other students who were already doing after school lessons to help them improve in their weak subject areas. Ade's dad also told the principal that he would like his son to be active in sports activities in the school. "My only challenge is that this may distract him from his academics."

"Don't worry," the principal said, "I will tell your son that to be fully accepted in any of the school's sporting events, he has to score a minimum of 60%, or he will be kicked out of sports." This idea sounded good to Ade's father.

Later in the evening, Ade's father invited him to his study. "Ade listen to me carefully. I have registered you for extra lessons in school. You also have my permission to do sporting activities in school, but on one condition. I must see an improvement in your academics. This is costing me money. I hope I won't regret this decision."

Ade could not contain his joy. "Thank you, daddy. You won't regret it. I will do my best to make you proud."

Ade ran out of his father's presence with tears of joy. He loved sports and his father had banned him from sports because of his poor performance in school. He was not even allowed to play a game of soccer with his friends on the street. "I will really need to work hard on my academics, so as to continue in the sports I love," he thought aloud.

When the new session began Ade would stay back in school to do extra lessons. He also joined the football club. He loved football and was a fast runner. After several weeks of coaching, his teacher reminded him that he would have to score up to 60% at the end of the term or leave the football club.

Ade was determined. He was finally happy and would make every sacrifice to play football. The weeks of extra lesson showed him that the subjects he struggled with were not difficult. He only needed to do extra studies on them. By the mid-term, Ade had an average of 61% in all his subjects. He was elated. This meant that he could remain in sports. By the end of the first term, Ade had an average of 65% in all his subjects.

"I am proud of you son," his father said. "Now, you can see that you can achieve anything if you set your mind to it."

The second term came, and it was time for the school's inter-house sports. Ade was in Blue house. Ade was not only playing football for his house, but he was also running as well. He was on the relay team and participating in the relay race.

The students practiced hard and the day of the inter house sports arrived. Ade's parents, siblings and his grandmother attended the event.

Ade remembered his grandmother's words and decided to do his best to stand out in all he participated in. At the end of the event, Blue house came first in football, and in all the running events. Ade and his team were called out to receive their medals. After getting 3 medals for football, relay and the 100 meters race, Ade was given the final medal as the sports man of the day. The principal called out his name for the final medal and Ade squared his shoulders and walked out proudly amidst cheers and applause from the crowd. His parents and grandmother also went out with him. His father was given the medal to put around his son's neck. He already had the three medals he had earlier won hanging on his neck. As Ade bowed for his father to put the medal on his neck, tears of joy streamed down his face. Though his father tried, he could not also hold back his tears of joy, as he placed the medal around his son's neck. "Son, thank you for making me proud," he said.

Ade smiled and looked at his grandmother who also had tears streaming down her face. He walked up to his grandmother and hugged her, "I made it Mami. I made it."

"Yes, you did my son. You did not only excel, but you also shone."

Moral of the story

We all have different talents and destinies. Never compare yourself with something else, but rather, work hard and shine in your own chosen field. Wherever you find yourself, always put your best foot forward.

Milton Keynes UK
Ingram Content Group UK Ltd.
UKHW021938281024
450365UK00018B/1161